OCTONAUTS ™

and the Great Christmas Rescue!

SIMON AND SCHUSTER

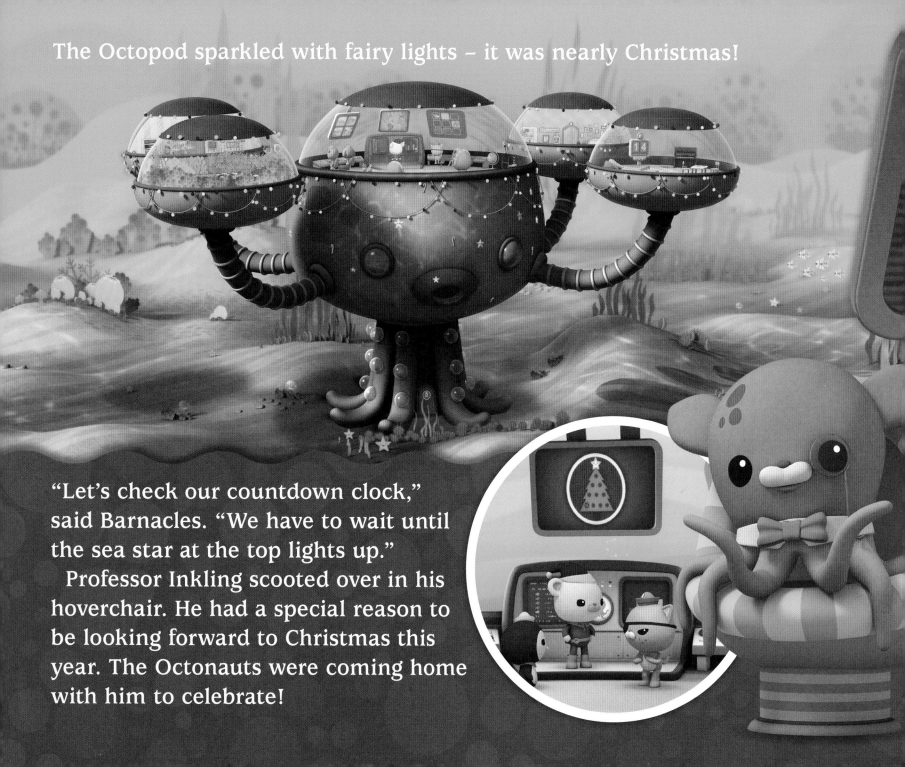

The Octopod sparkled with fairy lights – it was nearly Christmas!

"Let's check our countdown clock," said Barnacles. "We have to wait until the sea star at the top lights up."

Professor Inkling scooted over in his hoverchair. He had a special reason to be looking forward to Christmas this year. The Octonauts were coming home with him to celebrate!

Dashi tapped a computer screen and a picture appeared of Professor Inkling with his nephew, Squirt.

"He looks just like you," remarked Barnacles.

Inkling pointed to a photo of a giant rock.

"This is where Squirt lives and I grew up," he explained. "The seamount."

"It looks like a huge undersea mountain," cooed Peso.

Shellington nodded. "That's just what a seamount is!"

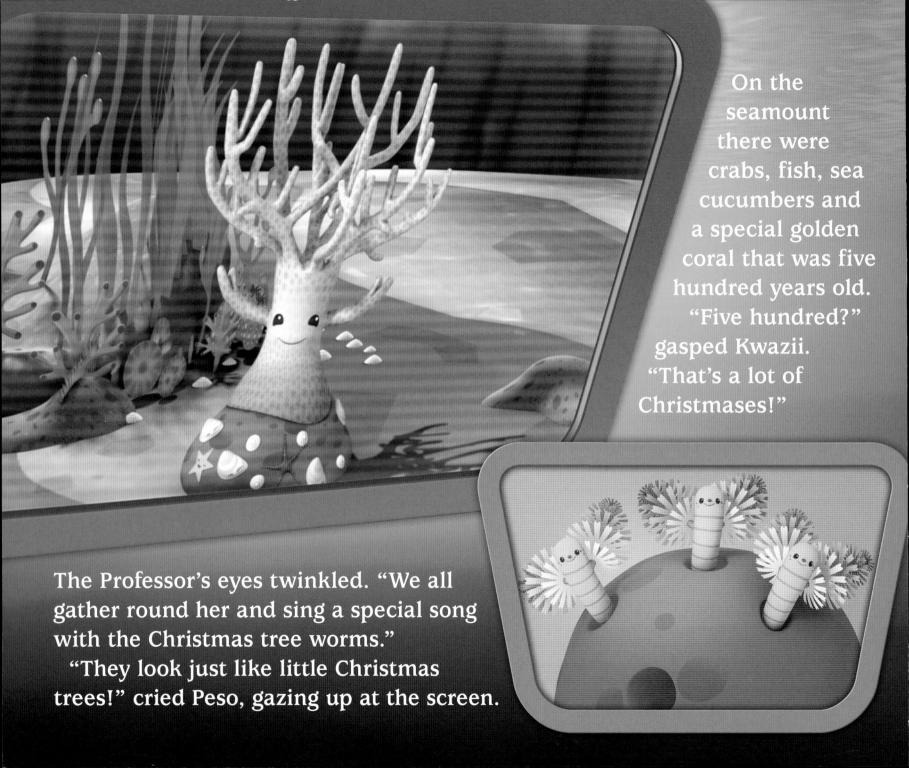

On the seamount there were crabs, fish, sea cucumbers and a special golden coral that was five hundred years old. "Five hundred?" gasped Kwazii. "That's a lot of Christmases!"

The Professor's eyes twinkled. "We all gather round her and sing a special song with the Christmas tree worms."

"They look just like little Christmas trees!" cried Peso, gazing up at the screen.

Barnacles checked the Christmas countdown clock one more time. If the Octonauts were going to reach the seamount before the big day, they needed to get moving!

"Dashi," he commanded. "Activate launch!"

The Octopod pulled in its pods and began to glide through the ocean.

Down in the launch bay, Tweak was too busy to think about celebrating. She had a top secret project to build!

"I've got to finish this surprise in time for Christmas," she puffed. "Hand me another hammer, Tunip!"

Tweak's hammering and drilling echoed all the way up the Octochute.

"I wonder what she's making?" said Peso.

"Don't know, matey," replied Kwazii. "She won't let anybody down there." The Captain chuckled. They'd just have to wait until Christmas to find out what Tweak was up to!

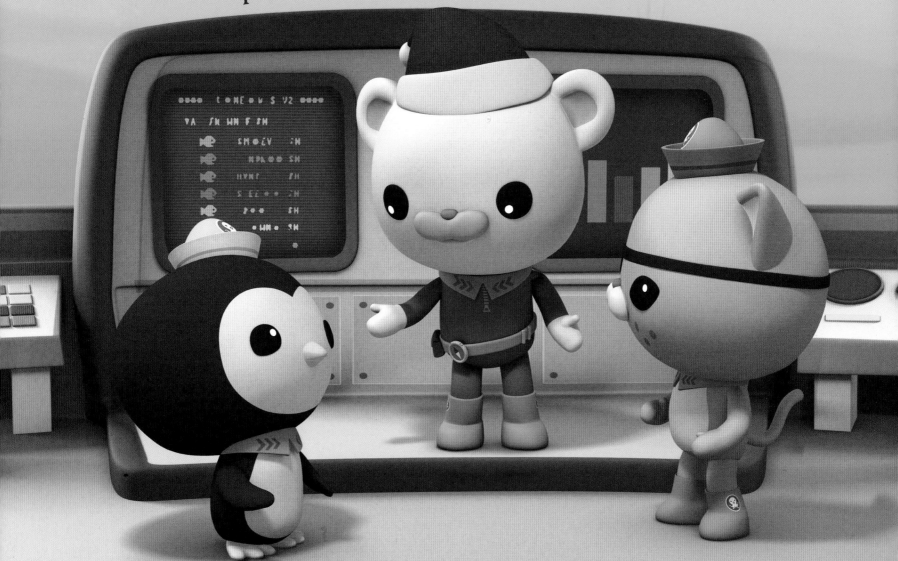

The crew had lots to do before Christmas. Peso gave Captain Barnacles a lesson in present wrapping. Kwazii helped trim the tree in the garden pod. When a bauble bounced into the Octochute, Kwazii slid down after it.

"Got it!" he cried, landing in the launch bay.

"What in the seven seas is that?" he gasped.

A giant red machine bobbed in the water – Tweak's gift for the Captain! "I call it the GUP-X," she grinned. "It's the toughest gup I've ever built!"

"That is the best present ever," whistled Kwazii, promising not to spoil the surprise.

The Octopod's voyage was nearly over. "There's the seamount, Captain!" cried Dashi. **Rattle! Boom!** The vessel shuddered and shook.

Dashi looked through the Octoscope. "There's been some kind of rockslide," she announced.

"All of those rocks must have fallen from the top of the seamount to the bottom," frowned the Captain.

Dashi spun round in her chair. "That means that the Professor's friends and family are trapped underneath!"

"Oh no!" cried Professor Inkling. "Squirt!"

"We'll find your nephew," promised Barnacles.

"Sound the Octoalert!"

"Octonauts, to the launch bay!"

The Octonauts had to get the sea creatures out from under the rock pile and move them to a safe place. Professor Inkling requested permission to join the rescue. His friends and family needed him!

"Agreed," said Barnacles. "This mission is going to take all of us working together."

Tweak prepared GUPs A, B, C, D, and E for launch.

The subs rushed to the rockslide.

"Oh my," sighed the Professor. "It's even bigger than we'd thought."

Captain Barnacles put a hand on his shoulder.

"On my honour as an Octonaut," he promised, "we'll search rock by rock until we find Squirt and all of your friends. Let's do this!"

The Octonauts leapt into action. Peso set up a treatment table. It was time to use his super speedy bandaging skills!

Tweak switched the GUP-D to crab mode and began to lift away boulders. Slowly and surely, sea creatures started to escape through the gaps in the rocks.

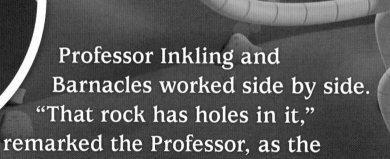

Professor Inkling and Barnacles worked side by side. "That rock has holes in it," remarked the Professor, as the Christmas tree worms popped out!

"Is it Christmas yet?" they chorused.

Barnacles checked his countdown clock. The worms still had a little while to wait.

Kwazii zoomed around the rockslide in the GUP-B, picking up hurt sea creatures. He found a crab with a sore claw and his urchin pal, but there was no sign of Inkling's nephew, Squirt.

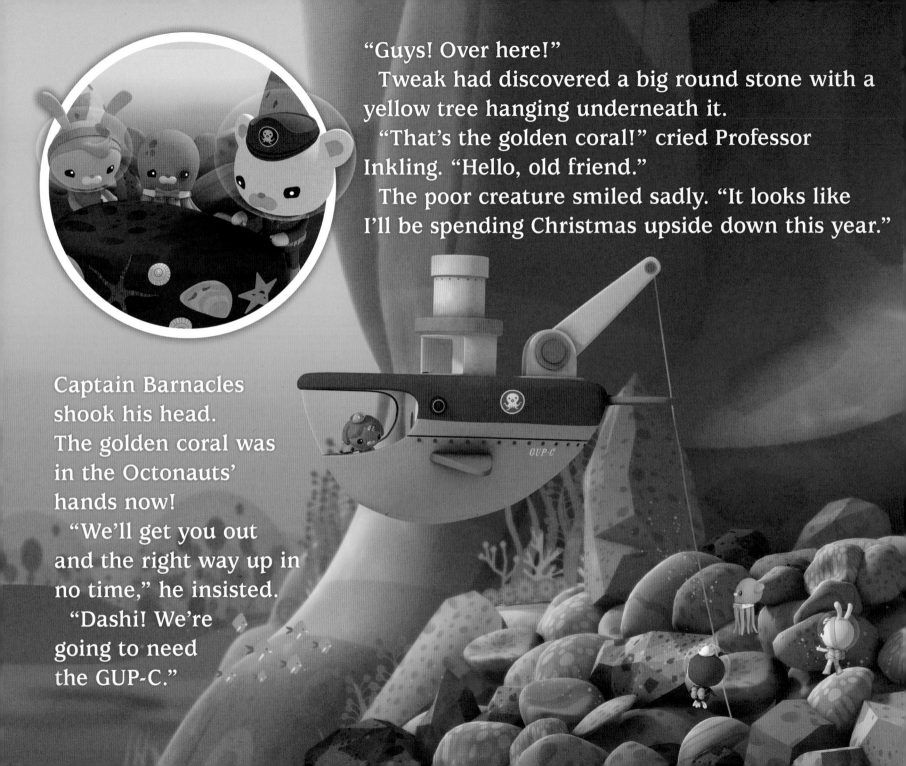

"Guys! Over here!"

Tweak had discovered a big round stone with a yellow tree hanging underneath it.

"That's the golden coral!" cried Professor Inkling. "Hello, old friend."

The poor creature smiled sadly. "It looks like I'll be spending Christmas upside down this year."

Captain Barnacles shook his head. The golden coral was in the Octonauts' hands now!

"We'll get you out and the right way up in no time," he insisted.

"Dashi! We're going to need the GUP-C."

The crew tied a towline around the base of the golden coral. Dashi got ready to winch the creature out of the rockslide.

"On my signal," ordered Barnacles. "One... two... three!"

The GUP-C rattled and cranked as it reeled in the towline. When the golden coral was free, Barnacles and Kwazii carefully pushed her the right way up.

The golden coral stretched out her branches and three baby sea snails appeared.

"Thanks for getting me out in one piece," she beamed. "These snails rely on me for protection."

Now only Squirt was missing.

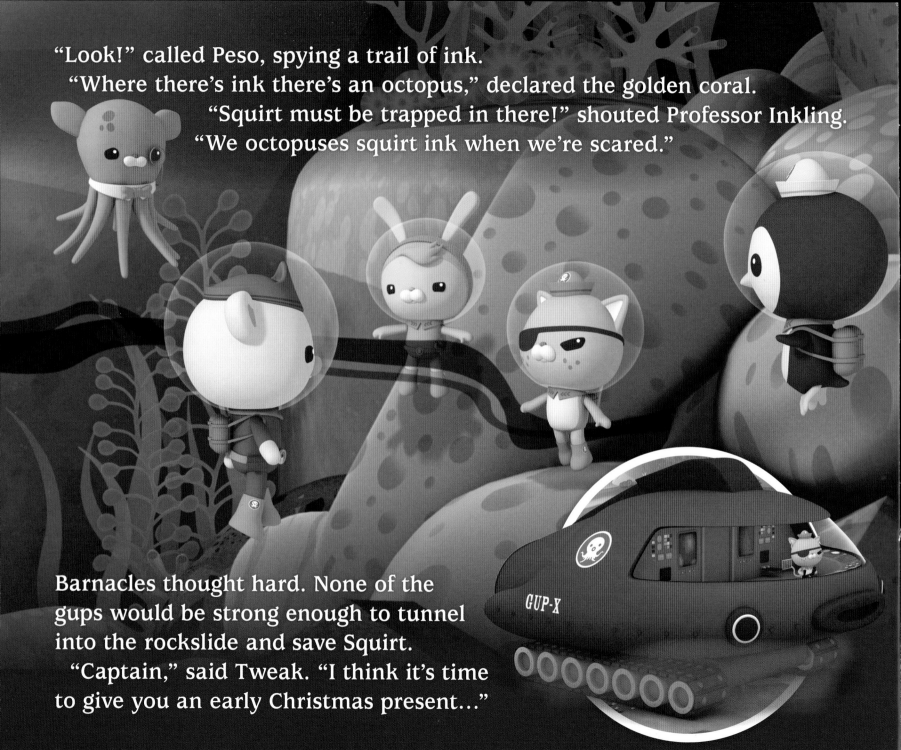

"Look!" called Peso, spying a trail of ink.
"Where there's ink there's an octopus," declared the golden coral.
"Squirt must be trapped in there!" shouted Professor Inkling.
"We octopuses squirt ink when we're scared."

Barnacles thought hard. None of the gups would be strong enough to tunnel into the rockslide and save Squirt.
"Captain," said Tweak. "I think it's time to give you an early Christmas present..."

GUP-X

The brand new GUP-X zoomed into view.
It had awesome caterpillar tracks and a super-
hard shell. It was the **toughest** gup ever!
Captain Barnacles couldn't wait to get driving.
"Thank you!" he grinned. "This is the perfect
Christmas gift at the perfect time."

The GUP-X powered through the rockslide in seconds. When the super-sub hit a dead-end, Kwazii swam out to search the cave.

"More ink!" he gasped, following a curling black trail.

A jet of ink sploshed right into Kwazii's face. He had found Squirt!

"Sorry," whimpered the young octopus. "I'm a little scared."

Crash!

Bang!

Boom!

Rocks and boulders began to crash down into the cave.

"Shiver me whiskers!" yowled Kwazii. "The tunnel's falling apart!"

Barnacles opened the gup's exit hatch so that Kwazii and Squirt could crawl in.

"Let's get out of here," he shouted.

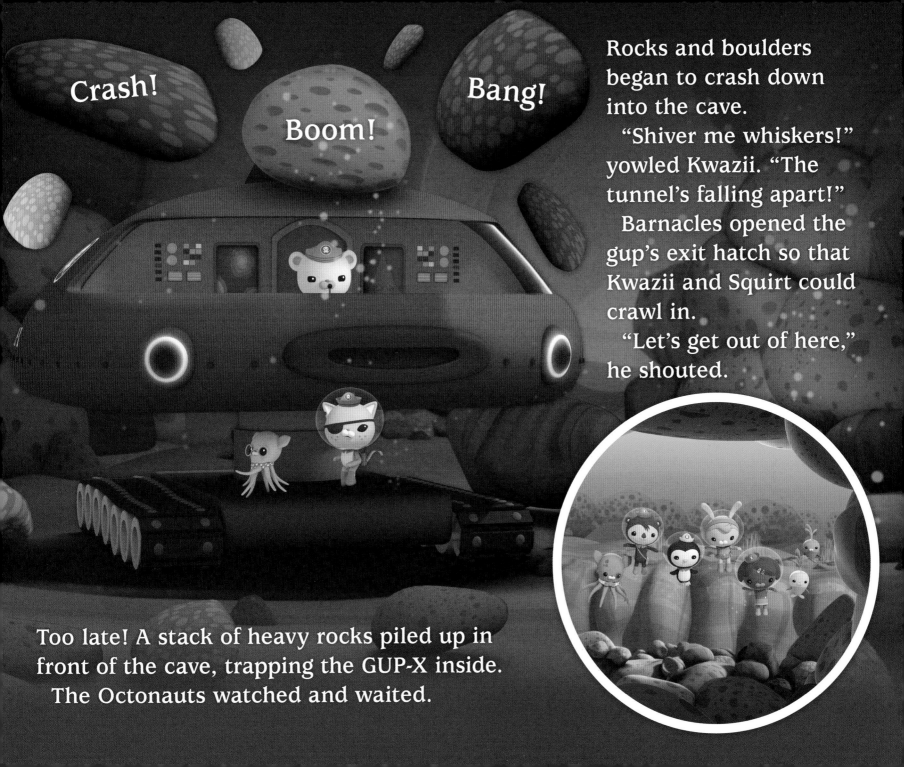

Too late! A stack of heavy rocks piled up in front of the cave, trapping the GUP-X inside. The Octonauts watched and waited.

Crash!

Boom!

Bang!

The GUP-X crashed its way out, sending rocks tumbling in all directions. The Octonauts cheered.

"Uncle Inkling!" cried Squirt, rushing up to give the Professor a hug.

"The gang's all here now," announced the golden coral. "Squirt was the last creature missing!"

Now that everyone was safe, they needed a new home.

"The best place would be at the top of the seamount," suggested Professor Inkling, "but there are dangerous waters along the way."

Peso gulped. None of the usual gups would make such a steep climb.

"I fitted special Octo-suction tyres to the GUP-X," said Tweak. "They should stick to the seamount no matter how fast the water is moving!"

"Everybody ready up there?" asked Captain Barnacles a little later.
The GUP-X began to slowly trundle up the rock face. Peso sat tight in the back. It was his job to keep an eye on the very littlest sea creatures!
"We've passed the rockslide!" said Kwazii.
Rough water began to swirl and bubble around the GUP-X. It was time to operate the sub's Octo-suction tyres!

Tweak had done a great job – the tyres were working perfectly! The seamount got steeper and steeper.

"Hold on," warned the Captain. "Let's give these Octo-suction tyres a real test."

The GUP-X trundled up an over-hanging rock.

"Woah!" cried the Octonauts, as the sub turned upside down! The GUP-X's tyres clung onto the rock face like glue.

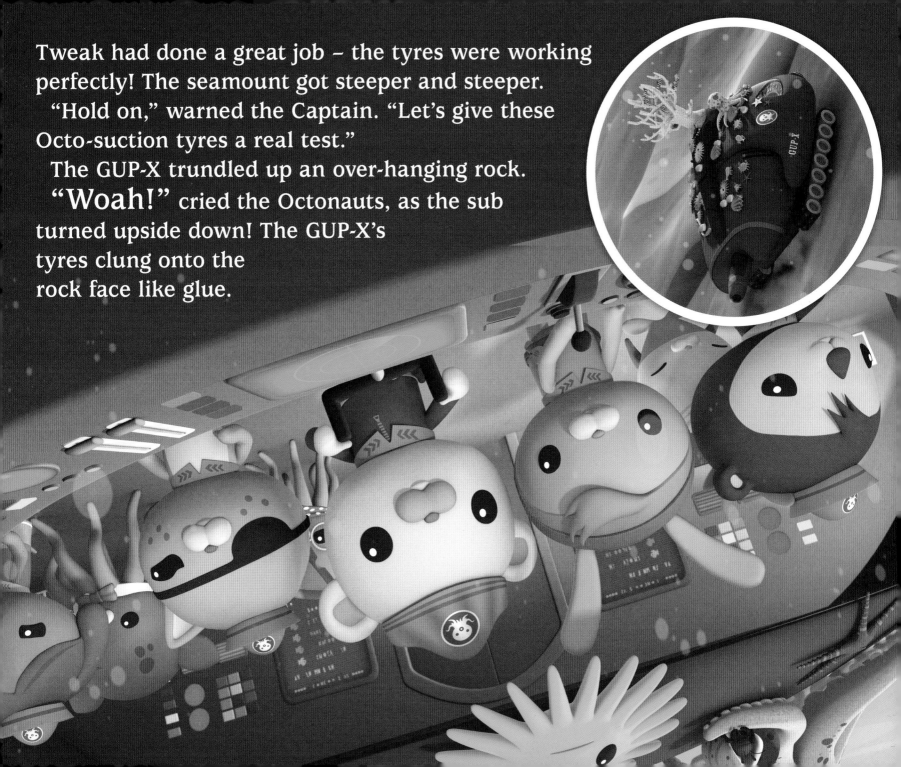

The sub was almost at the top at the seamount.

"This last climb is going to be tough," warned Barnacles. "Everyone hold on tight."

The little sea snails nestled even deeper into the golden coral's branches.

"We're ready, Captain!"

Suddenly disaster struck.

"Octonauts!" cried the golden coral.

"Sea snail overboard!"

"I'll help you!" shouted Kwazii, pulling on his diving helmet.

Kwazii swam out and got the sea snail, but then the current got Kwazii! The brave pirate cat couldn't paddle back to the GUP-X.

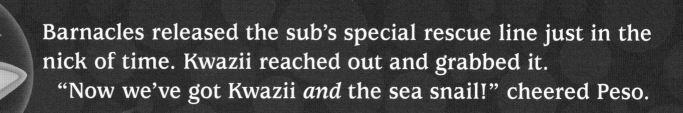

Barnacles released the sub's special rescue line just in the
nick of time. Kwazii reached out and grabbed it.
"Now we've got Kwazii *and* the sea snail!" cheered Peso.

"We're almost there," announced
Captain Barnacles, "but I don't think
we'll make it in time for Christmas."
  Tweak chuckled, then pointed to a
special green button.

"It activates slippery slime," she
explained.
  Kwazii cheered. The GUP-X could
use slime to slide down into the
middle of the seamount. Slime
sliding was just like sledging!

"We made it!" said Inkling, as the GUP-X slid to a stop. Peso hugged the Professor. "And we're all together."

"Is it Christmas yet?" trilled the little
Christmas tree worms.
    Captain Barnacles pulled out his countdown clock –
a happy star was twinkling at the top of the tree!

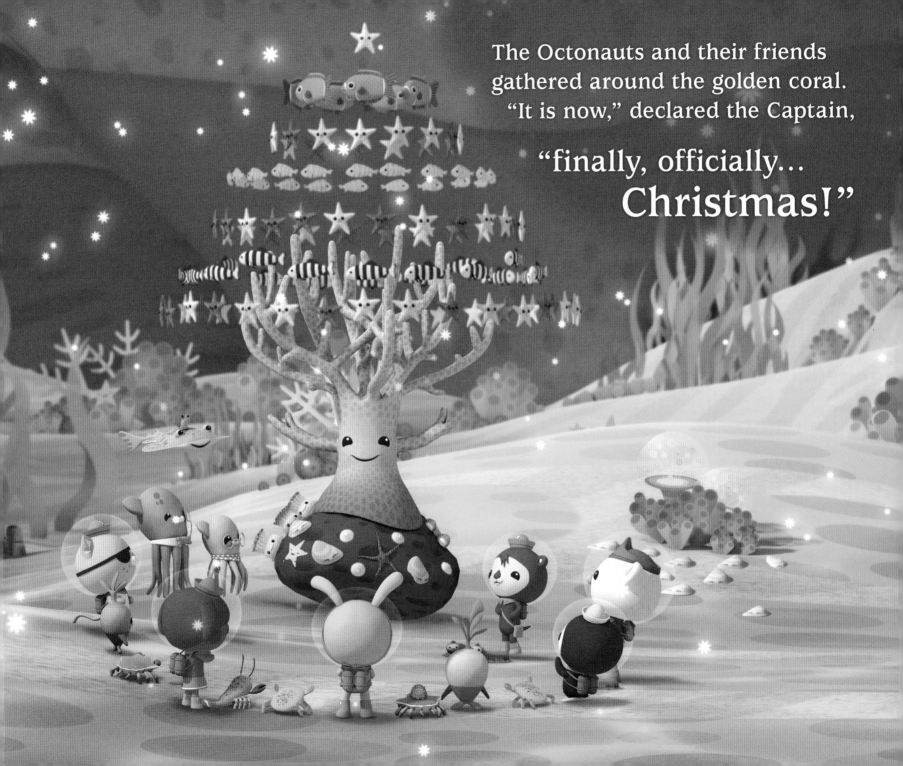

The Octonauts and their friends
gathered around the golden coral.
"It is now," declared the Captain,

"finally, officially...
Christmas!"

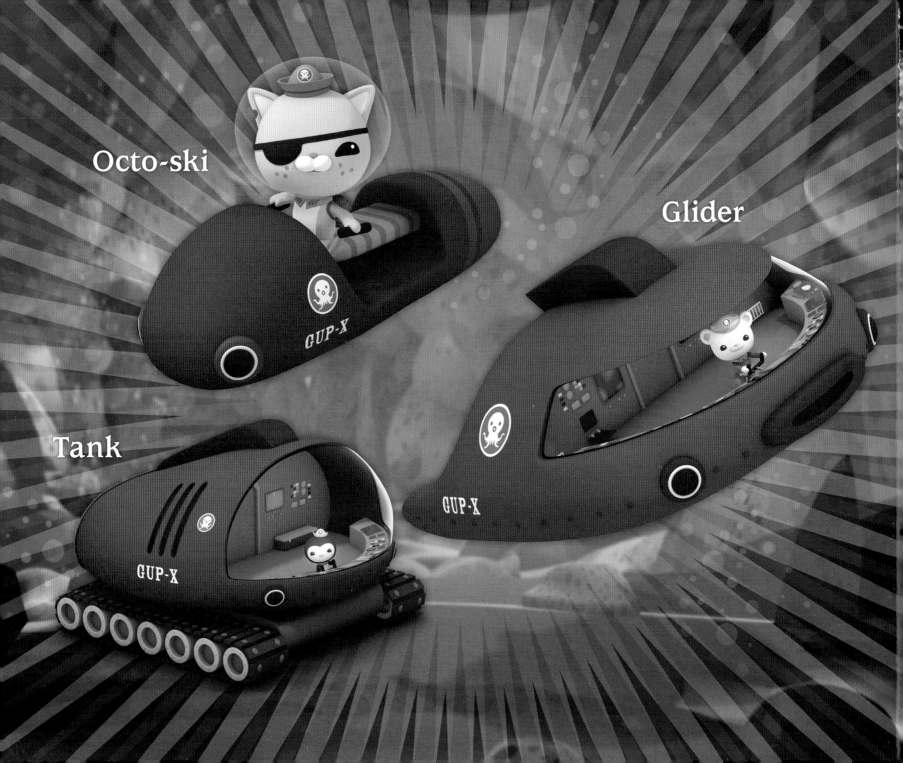

Octo-ski

Glider

Tank